You can be a
Brownie Girl Scout, too!

If you are 6, 7, or 8 years old, or in the 1st, 2nd, or 3rd grade, just ask your parents to look in your local telephone directory under "**Girl Scouts,**" and call for information. You can also ask your parents to call **Girl Scouts of the U.S.A.** at **1-(212) 852-8000** or write to 420 Fifth Avenue, New York, NY 10018-2702 to find out about becoming a Girl Scout in your area.

For Julianna,
who also likes to "do it self"—M.L.

For the two artists I admire most,
Mom and Dad—with love, L.S.L.

Copyright © 1996 by Girl Scouts of the United States of America. All rights reserved. Published by Grosset & Dunlap, Inc., a member of The Putnam & Grosset Group, New York, in cooperation with Girl Scouts of the United States of America. GROSSET & DUNLAP is a trademark of Grosset & Dunlap, Inc. Published simultaneously in Canada. Printed in the U.S.A.

Library of Congress Cataloging-in-Publication Data

Leonard, Marcia.
    Jo Ann and the surprise party / by Marcia Leonard ; illustrated by Laurie Struck Long.
        p.   cm. — (Here come the Brownies ; 11)
    "A Brownie Girl Scout Book."
    Summary: The Brownie troop is preparing a surprise party for their leader, and Jo Ann must decide whether to make her favorite Chinese dessert and risk being different from the other girls.
    [1. Girl Scouts—Fiction.   2. Chinese Americans—Fiction.   3. Individuality—Fiction.]   I. Long, Laurie Struck, ill.   II. Title.   III. Series.
PZ7.L549Jo   1996
[Fic]—dc20   95-18332
                                                              CIP
ISBN 0-448-40884-8   AC
A B C D E F G H I J

HERE COME THE BROWNIES

A Brownie Girl Scout Book

Jo Ann and the Surprise Party

By Marcia Leonard
Illustrated by Laurie Struck Long

Grosset & Dunlap • New York
In association with GIRL SCOUTS OF THE U.S.A.

1

"La, la, la," everyone sang at the Friday Brownie Girl Scout meeting. "La, la, la, la, laaaaa."

Jo Ann tried not to giggle. But twenty-five girls going la-la-la did sound pretty funny!

"Okay!" said their leader Mrs. Quinones. "Now that you know the tune to our new song, we can add the words." She handed each girl a sheet of paper.

Jo Ann stared at it in surprise. "Mrs. Q.!

This looks like a fill-in-the-blank test," she said.

Mrs. Q. smiled. "It's not a test. But you do get to fill in the blanks. When you finish, you will have written your very own song."

She handed out pencils. "Each of you is special. And each of you is different. So your songs will be different, too."

Jo Ann bent over her paper. "Jo Ann's Song," she wrote at the top. Then she started filling in the other spaces.

___Jo Ann___ 's SONG

My name is _Jo Ann_.
I am _7_ years old.
I have my own story,
And here it's told.
Carson St. is where I live,
I am _____ inches high.

Jo Ann stopped writing. "Mrs. Q.?" she called out. "I don't know how tall I am."

"Me either," said Corrie.

"No problem," said Mrs. Q. "I brought a tape measure. You can measure each other."

Amy was first in line. Corrie tried to read the tape measure for her.

"Amy! Hold still," she said. "You're wiggling so much, I can't read the numbers."

Marsha giggled. "That's because she's standing on her tiptoes."

Amy laughed and stood flat on her feet. "Sorry! I'm already the youngest in class. I didn't want to be the shortest, too."

"No chance. I'm shorter than you," said Corrie. "But it doesn't matter. Remember what Mrs. Q. said. We're all different. And that's okay."

Marsha and Lauren nodded. But Jo Ann wasn't so sure. She was glad she wasn't the shortest—or the tallest. She didn't like being *too* different. It made her feel funny.

As soon as Jo Ann got measured, she went back to work on her song.

I am __**51**__ inches high.
My nose is right here on my face,
And __**brown**__ is the color of my eyes.

Lauren pointed to the next line of the song. "Here's an easy one," she said. "My favorite food is..."

"Chocolate anything!" Amy said quickly.

"Pepperoni pizza!" said Lauren.

"Peanut butter and banana on a toasted raisin bagel!" said Krissy A. Then she

grinned. "I guess that won't fit on the line. I'd better just write peanut butter."

"My favorite is brownies—because I am one!" Krissy S. giggled. "How about you, Jo Ann?"

"Oh, I don't know," Jo Ann replied. But really, she *did* know. Her favorite was almond dofu, a special Chinese dessert that she and her grandmother made together. Only she didn't want to say so. It was too…different.

"I guess brownies are my favorite, too," she said. She did like brownies a lot. Just not as much as almond dofu.

The girls finished their songs. Then they took turns singing them out loud. As Jo Ann listened, she learned all kinds of new things about her friends. Krissy A.'s favorite game was computer checkers. Lauren's was socccer. A first grader named Lucy knew sign language. And Krissy S. could do cartwheels.

Krissy even did one in the middle of her song. And she made a big curtsy at the end, as if she had on a fancy ball gown instead of her Brownie uniform.

Krissy's such an actress, thought Jo Ann. She loves standing out in a crowd. Not like me.

Marsha was next. Then it was Jo Ann's turn. She started out fine. But when she came to "My favorite food is brownies," her voice wobbled. Luckily, no one seemed to notice, and she finished the song okay. But even so, she felt funny—as if she'd told a little lie.

10

2

When everyone finished singing, Mrs. Q. stood up. "Your songs are one way to tell about yourselves," she said. "Next week, we'll try another way. It's a time line. Who knows what that is?"

Jo Ann raised her hand. "My big sister Allison made one in school," she said. "It showed important dates in history."

"Right," said Mrs. Q. "The one you make will be like that. But it will show important dates in *your* lives."

MOVED TO NEW HOUSE 1955

GRADUATED HIGH SCHOOL 1967

WORKED IN MEXICO 1972

FIRST CAR

BORN 1950 NOVEMBER 27

1963 JUNIOR TENNIS CHAMP

1971 GRADUATED COLLEGE

TRIP TO HAWAII

1973 MARRIED

She unfolded an extra-long piece of paper. "This is my time line," she said. "See? I marked off each year of my life. Then I wrote down the special things I did over the years. And I drew some pictures to go with them. You can do the same with the special things *you* have done."

"You mean like the time I got to dance in the Nutcracker?" asked Marsha. "That was really special to me."

"How about the day I got my puppy, Muffin?" said Sarah.

"Or the day my baby sister was born!" said Lauren.

"Sure," said Mrs. Q. "Anybody else?"

"My first Brownie meeting," said Corrie. "I was so nervous. But it turned out great."

"My second Brownie camp-out!" said Amy. "Remember? I got sick and threw up!" She held her stomach and rolled her eyes.

"Time lines can show good things *and* not-so-good things," said Mrs. Q. "Make a list of the things you have done that are important to you. If you want, ask your families for help. Next Friday, you can fill in your time lines."

Jo Ann couldn't wait to get started on

her list. She decided to look
up some dates in her
baby book. Then if she
had any questions, she
would ask Nai-Nai, her

grandmother. Nai-Nai had lived with Jo
Ann's family ever since Yeh-Yeh—Jo Ann's
grandfather—had died. And she had a great
memory.

Mrs. Q. checked her watch. "Speaking of
time, ours is nearly up! I'll put my time line
on the table. You can take a look later, if
you like."

The Brownies got together for their
friendship squeeze. Then Jo Ann, Amy, and
Krissy S. went to see Mrs. Q.'s time line.

"Cool! It's a history of Mrs. Q.," said
Amy. She pointed to a date. "Look! She was
a junior tennis champ! I didn't know that."

"And she worked in Mexico for a year," said Krissy S. "I didn't know that, either."

Then Jo Ann noticed something. Mrs. Q.'s birthday was just eight days away! Suddenly she got the greatest idea....

We should have a birthday party for her, she thought. Or better yet, a *surprise* birthday party!

She opened her mouth to tell the other girls. Then she shut it—fast. Mrs. Q. was standing nearby. What if she heard? That would wreck the surprise.

Jo Ann felt like a bubble ready to pop. She pulled Amy and Krissy S. over to the water fountain.

"Guess what!" she whispered. "Mrs. Q.'s birthday is next Saturday! I think we should give her a surprise party."

"Wow! What a great idea," said Krissy.

"We could do it next Friday—right after the meeting. That way, we'd be together already."

"Yeah," said Amy. "But can we have it someplace besides the school lunchroom? It always smells like leftovers in here." She pinched her nose. "Pee-yew!"

"How about my house?" offered Jo Ann.

"Great!" said Amy. "Let's do it!"

"Do what?" It was Mrs. Q.

Amy's jaw dropped. For once she didn't have anything to say.

"Uh—do our time lines," Krissy said quickly. "We think it's going to be fun."

Mrs. Q. gave them a funny look. Then she got a drink of water and walked away.

"Whew! That was close!" Jo Ann whispered. "Let's call everyone tonight. If it's okay with our parents, we can meet at my house tomorrow. Then we can plan you-know-what without you-know-who hearing all about it!"

3

Jo Ann looked at the clock on her desk.
"Oops! I'd better hurry," she said to herself.
"The Brownies will be here any minute."

She ran down to the kitchen to look for
some snacks. Her grandmother was sitting
at the table drinking jasmine tea and
sketching in her notebook. Nai-Nai designed
clothes. She was always jotting down ideas.
And she always wore great outfits, too.

Jo Ann loved what Nai-Nai had on
today. Dark blue pants. A long matching

jacket. And a silk vest with a pretty
butterfly pattern.

Jo Ann stroked her grandmother's sleeve.
"Is this one of your new designs?" she
asked. "I really like the vest!"

"Me, too," said Nai-Nai. "The style is
new and American. But the butterfly pattern
is Chinese—and very old. Butterflies mean
joy."

"They do look happy," said Jo Ann. She opened a cabinet and got out some pretzels and graham crackers. The crinkle of the bags woke up her pet parrot, Cookie.

"Where's the chow? Where's the chow?" he squawked.

Leave it to Cookie. A brass band could march by his cage and he would still sleep through it. But just try to get out some food without waking him up!

"Forget it, Cookie!" Jo Ann told him. "This is people food. Not parrot food."

"Are you hungry, Jo Ann? I can fix you something," offered her grandmother.

Jo Ann smiled. Nai-Nai was a super cook. "No thanks. I was just getting snacks ready for the Brownies."

"I could fix something special for them," said her grandmother. "Scallion pancakes or steamed dumplings? Some shrimp toast?"

Jo Ann's mouth watered. But she shook her head. "It's okay, Nai-Nai. This will be fine."

Jo Ann felt a little bad about turning down her grandmother. But there was no way she was serving Chinese food for snack. No one else in Brownies ever did anything like that!

Just then the doorbell rang. It was Corrie—with a great big cardboard box.

"Art supplies. For making party decorations," Corrie explained as they trooped down to the basement.

She emptied the box onto the floor. Out spilled markers, scissors, bags of sequins and glitter, feathers, ribbons, and lots of colored paper. Corrie had everything!

The other girls arrived a few minutes later. Soon they were all sitting on the floor, cutting, pasting, folding, and coloring.

Jo Ann cut fancy paper into strips to make chains. "We can write a Brownie's name on each strip," she told Krissy S. "Then the chains will be like us holding hands in our Brownie ring."

"Ooh, Mrs. Q. will like that," Krissy said.

"Hey, you guys," said Marsha. "What are we going to give Mrs. Q. for a present?"

"How about in-line skates?" said Amy. "That's what I want for *my* birthday."

"Very funny." Krissy A. grinned. "I think

it should have something to do with Brownies."

"Something we make ourselves," said Corrie.

"How about a memory book?" said Lauren. "We could fill an album with pictures from our meetings and camp-outs and stuff."

"Cool!" said Amy. "I vote yes."

So did the other girls.

"Okay," said Krissy S. "What about food?"

"I've got pretzels and graham crackers right here," said Jo Ann.

Krissy S. laughed. "I meant food for the party! My dad and I make great birthday cakes. We can make one for Mrs. Q. But what else should we have?"

"Well, what if we each bring our favorite party food?" said Corrie.

"Sure," said Sarah. "I could bring vegetables and dip."

"I'll bring English muffin pizzas," said Lauren.

"And I'll make..." Jo Ann paused. "My favorite is..." Oh, no! It was the same problem she'd had writing her song. She wanted to say almond dofu. She and Nai-Nai made it for all their family parties. But once again she felt too embarrassed.

"Oh, I don't know," she said at last. "I can't decide."

"Hey! Usually it's Marsha who can't make up her mind," teased Lauren.

Marsha laughed. "Oh, be quiet, Lauren," she teased back.

"How about brownies, Jo Ann?" said

Sarah. "You said in your song that brownies were your favorite."

Jo Ann felt trapped by her own words. "I do like brownies," she said slowly. "But my *real* favorite is...um...almond dofu."

"Toe what?" said Amy.

"Tofu," said Corrie. "It's that wobbly white stuff, right, Jo Ann?"

"Right. I mean, wrong. I mean, almond dofu isn't really tofu. It's a yummy Chinese dessert." Jo Ann tried to explain. "See, you make this pudding. It's kind of like almond Jell-O. Then you cut it up. And you put it in a special syrup. Then you add some fruit... and..."

Jo Ann's voice trailed off. The other girls were looking at her blankly, and she felt weird. As if she were from another planet, or something.

"Never mind," she said. "I'll make brownies." Then she quickly changed the subject. "That sign looks good, you guys."

"Thanks," said Corrie. She and Sarah held up the banner they had made. It said, "HAPPY BIRTHDAY MRS. Q!" in rainbow letters. And it was decorated with glitter, stars, and shiny paper hearts.

"Hey! Look at these cool party hats," said Amy. She modeled one that had yellow feathers sprouting from the top.

"Cute!" said Jo Ann.

Krissy A. took a handful of pretzels. "There's one thing we haven't figured out

yet," she said. "How are we going to get Mrs. Q. to the party?"

"Let's ask Mr. Q. to bring her over," said Lauren. "We could call him right now."

"Okay," said Jo Ann. She picked up the phone. Then she quickly put it down. "Wait! What if *Mrs. Q.* answers!"

"Maybe you could ask her something about your time line," said Marsha.

Jo Ann nodded. "Okay. Here goes!" She held her breath as the phone rang. Once. Twice. Three times.

"Hello?"

It was Mr. Q.! Jo Ann gave the Brownies

27

the thumbs-up sign. But as she talked to Mr. Q., she started to frown. Then she turned her thumb down.

"That's okay. I understand," she said. "If you get back in time, please come to the party anyway." She hung up the phone.

"Bad news?" asked Sarah.

Jo Ann nodded. "He can't do it. He has to pick up their daughter Nina from college. She's coming home for Mrs. Q.'s birthday."

"So much for that plan," said Corrie. "Now what are we going to do?"

Jo Ann thought hard for a moment. "I know!" she said finally. "I have an idea that just might work...."

4

"Check out these pictures!" Amy said at lunch on Tuesday. "They're for Mrs. Q.'s memory book."

Jo Ann put down her apple and took the stack from Amy. "Wow! These are great!" she said. "That's us at the toy museum. And there we are at the children's hospital."

Jo Ann passed the pictures on to Corrie. Then she reached into her backpack. "I brought a picture, too," she said. "It's Mrs.

Q. on our first camp-out. Remember? It rained every single day."

The girls crowded around to see. There was Mrs. Q. in a bright yellow slicker and hat. Her arms were out. Her head was tipped back. And she had a big grin on her face.

Lauren laughed. "That's Mrs. Q. all right! She can smile even when it's pouring rain."

"It's perfect!" said Amy. "We'll put it on the first page."

"Here's something else for Mrs. Q.," said Corrie. "It's a birthday card I made." She held up a paper doll. It was dressed like a Brownie and it was holding a sign that said, "Happy Birthday from Your Brownie Troop."

"That is so cool!" said Marsha.

"Wait. Here's the best part." Corrie unfolded the card. It was a whole string of Brownie paper dolls! "There's one for every girl in the troop to write a message on."

"Can I be first?" asked Amy.

"Sure," said Corrie.

✳   ✳   ✳

After school, Jo Ann's mom took Jo Ann, Sarah, Krissy S., and Corrie to the party store.

"The paper plates and napkins are in the back," said Jo Ann's mom. "Why don't you go find something you like? I'll be right here, looking at cards."

The girls hurried to the back of the store.

"How about these plates?" asked Sarah. "They've got puppies and kittens on them."

"Cute," said Krissy. "But not for Mrs. Q. What about these blue ones?"

"Pretty color," said Corrie. "But kind of plain."

They looked around some more. There was so much to choose from! But nothing was quite right for Mrs. Q.

Then they saw them! The plates looked as if they were sprinkled with confetti. They even had the word SURPRISE! written on them.

Sarah and Krissy S. picked up two packages of plates. And Jo Ann picked up the matching napkins.

"We're all set," she said. "Let's go get my mom."

They were almost at the front of the store, when they heard a familiar voice.

It was Mrs. Q.! She was talking to Jo Ann's mother!

The girls ran back down the aisle. Quickly they put the plates and napkins on a shelf. Then they ducked behind a big bunch of balloons and crouched down.

"Did she see us?" Krissy whispered.

"I don't think so," Sarah replied.

"Hello, girls!" a voice said behind them.

"Mrs. Q.!" Jo Ann was so startled, she jumped back. She almost knocked over the whole balloon display. "What...what are you doing here?" she asked.

"Just buying some cards," said Mrs. Q. "What about you girls?

Are you playing hide-and-seek?"

"Uh—kind of." Jo Ann got to her feet. "But I think we're done now. Right, guys?"

Her friends nodded hard.

"Well, I just wanted to say hi. I have to run," said Mrs. Q. "See you Friday."

The girls watched her leave the store.

"Talk about bad timing!" said Krissy.

"Really!" said Sarah. "But I don't think she guessed anything."

Jo Ann's mom came over. "Well, girls, I think your secret is still safe," she said. "But there is one little problem. I told Mrs. Q. we were just stopping on the way to get ice cream. So we'd better pay for our things and get over to Mr. Freezy's." She grinned. "You girls don't mind, do you?"

"No way!" said the Brownies. "Let's go!"

5

Today Jo Ann is 100 days old!
So we had her One Hundred Days
Ceremony. We put her on a blanket
and placed some things around her.
An abacus. A doll. A book. A set of
paints. Then we waited to see what
she picked first, to find out what
kind of person she will be.

When Allison had her ceremony,
she went straight for the doll. But
not Jo Ann! She ignored everything
we set out and reached for Nai-Nai's
silk blouse! Nai-Nai says this means

she will make beautiful clothes—like
her grandmother....

Jo Ann smiled. She put down her baby
book and turned to the list she was making
for her time line. "One Hundred Days
Ceremony," she wrote. Then she paged
through the book again, looking for more
ideas.

All week long, Jo Ann had been thinking
about the big events in her life. The day last
summer when she learned how to dive. The
time she and her family went to New York
City for Chinese New Year. The sleep-over
she had for her seventh birthday.

Now it was Thursday afternoon, and her
list was almost done. A good thing, too!
The Brownie meeting was tomorrow. And
so was the party!

There was a tap on Jo Ann's door, and

her grandmother looked in. "Are you ready to make brownies?" she asked.

"In a second, Nai-Nai. First listen to this. It's from my baby book...."

> Jo Ann made her first sentence today! She was building a block tower, and Allison tried to help—as usual. But Jo Ann had her own ideas. "No!" she said very loudly. "Jo Ann do it self!"

Nai-Nai laughed. "I remember that! You always wanted to do things your own way. You had strong feelings about nearly everything."

"Like what?" said Jo Ann. "Tell me, Nai-Nai. Please? I like to hear about when I was little."

"I'll tell you while we make the brownies," her grandmother promised.

Jo Ann jumped up and followed Nai-Nai to the kitchen. Nai-Nai tied an apron over her red dress. And she helped Jo Ann put one on, too. Then they started mixing the brownie batter.

"When you were little," said Nai-Nai, "you liked to arrange things yourself. You'd

stack up your books or line up your toys. And if anyone tried to change something, you got mad."

Jo Ann grinned. "I still feel that way about the stuff in my room."

"You wanted to pick out your own clothes, too," Nai-Nai went on. "And choose your own food from the serving dishes."

"Jo Ann do it self," said Jo Ann.

"Exactly! Feed *self*. Climb stairs *self*. Read book *self*." Nai-Nai smiled at her. "You've always been sure of what you wanted."

"Is that good?" asked Jo Ann. Lately she hadn't felt sure of things at all.

Her grandmother stirred chocolate chips into the batter. "*I* think so!" she said. "Maybe because I'm that way, too."

Jo Ann looked at her in surprise. "You are?"

"How do you think I ended up here?" said Nai-Nai. "My parents didn't want me to leave China. But I had my own ideas. I wanted to start my own clothing company—in America."

"And you did!" Jo Ann said. "Were you scared?"

Nai-Nai ruffled Jo Ann's hair. "Well, it was hard at first, being in a strange country. But I remember when I was learning English. I was in a classroom with people from all over the world. And I thought, how wonderful! We speak different languages. We like different foods. We dress differently. But we are all the same, too. We all want to be Americans."

Jo Ann remembered the songs her troop had made up at the last Brownie meeting. "Sometimes I'm different from my friends. And sometimes I'm the same," she said.

"Both are fine," said Nai-Nai. "As long as you are true to yourself."

Jo Ann was quiet as they got the brownies ready for the oven. She thought about what her grandmother had said. And she decided that she had not been true to herself lately. About what she wanted to do. And how she felt. And what she liked.

"Nai-Nai," she said. "If there's time after dinner, could we make almond dofu? That's what I *really* want to have at the party!"

Her grandmother smiled. "We'll make time," she said.

6

"I'm so excited, I can hardly stand it," Jo Ann said as she headed for the lunchroom. "It's finally Friday. Finally time for Brownies."

"And the party!" said Marsha. "I can't believe everything's ready."

"Almost everything," said Corrie. "Two girls still need to sign the card. But they can do that at the meeting."

"Be careful!" warned Lauren. "We don't want Mrs. Q. to see it."

"And remember—no talking about the party in the lunchroom!" Amy added. "We have to act like this is just a regular Brownie meeting."

"Right!" said Jo Ann. She tried to wipe the grin off her face. But the minute she caught someone's eye, she started to giggle.

The other girls had the same problem—until they got to the lunchroom. Then they all stopped laughing. Except for the lunchroom monitor, the room was empty. There was no sign of Mrs. Q.!

"Where is she?" asked Marsha.

"Maybe she's just late," said Amy.

"But she's *never* late," moaned Jo Ann. "What if she's not coming?"

They sat down. One after the other, the rest of the Brownies and some of their moms arrived. But still no Mrs. Q.

Minutes ticked by, and the girls got very quiet. How could they have a party without Mrs. Q.?

Finally Jo Ann couldn't sit still anymore. "I'm going to the office," she said. "Maybe Mrs. Q. left a message there for us."

But just as she reached the door, it opened. And Mrs. Q. hurried in.

A big sigh of relief went around the room. The party was still on!

"Sorry, girls. I've been running late all day," Mrs. Q. said. "Let's make our Brownie ring quickly. Then we can get started on the time lines. I can't wait to see how they turn out!"

*   *   *

Jo Ann picked up a marker and started coloring another picture on her time line. This one was of her on the diving board. It was going okay. But she was having trouble keeping her mind on her picture.

She leaned over to talk to Krissy S. "This is fun," she said softly. "But I know something that will be even more fun!"

Krissy pretended to think hard. "What could it be? Give me a hint."

"It starts with a P and ends with a Y.

47

And there's some ART in between," said Jo Ann.

"Shhh! Mrs. Q. might hear you!" said Lauren.

But pretty soon everyone was whispering about the party.

"I'd better get the last two girls to sign the card," said Corrie.

When Mrs. Q. wasn't looking, she got up and went to sit with Lucy. A few minutes later, she got up again. This time she sat with Sharnelle.

Mrs. Q. turned around and spotted her. "Are you done with your time line, Corrie?" she asked.

Corrie hid the card behind her back.

"Um, not really," she said. She hurried to her seat.

"Whew!" said Jo Ann. "We'd better watch out. Or else Mrs. Q. will know something is going on."

But a few minutes later, Marsha came over to tell Jo Ann she was bringing fruit salad instead of grapes. Then more girls dashed back and forth, giggling and whispering.

"Girls! Girls!" called Mrs. Q. "What's going on? Don't you want to make time lines?"

Suddenly everybody looked guilty.

"Yes! We do!" the girls said.

"Maybe you need a break," said Mrs. Q. "Let's play a few games. Then you can go back to your drawing."

The troop played Red Light, Green Light

and Simon Says. But it did not help. They still had trouble paying attention—especially Jo Ann.

She kept thinking about the plan she and the other girls had come up with. When the meeting was over, it would be her job to keep Mrs. Q. in the lunchroom after the rest of the Brownies left. *And* get her to the party.

It all depends on me, thought Jo Ann. I hope I can do it.

Soon Amy's mom peeked through the door. Then more parents showed up and waited in the hall to pick up their kids.

Mrs. Q. looked at the clock in surprise. "It's early," she said. "But I guess we can wrap things up. We'll finish the time lines next week—okay?"

"Okay!" the girls said quickly.

They cleaned up in record time. Then they made a ring for their friendship squeeze.

"Good luck, Jo Ann! See you later at your house!" Krissy S. whispered as the circle broke up.

"Thanks," said Jo Ann. She sat down to wait. Before long she was the only Brownie left in the lunchroom.

"Do you have a ride, Jo Ann?" asked Mrs. Q.

"I think so. I mean, my mom *knows* I have Brownies on Fridays," said Jo Ann. Her voice sounded fake to her. She wished she were an actress, like Krissy S.

She stared at the clock. Time was passing so slowly!

"I'm sorry you have to wait, Mrs. Q.," she said.

"I don't mind," said Mrs. Q. "Your mom is probably just running late—the way I was today. I wanted to finish all my errands because my daughter Nina is coming home from college this weekend."

"She is?" Jo Ann tried to look surprised. "I bet you'll be glad to see her."

"I sure will!" said Mrs. Q.

Just then the school secretary poked her head through the door. "Mrs. Quinones?" she said. "Jo Ann's mother called. She's stuck at home. Can you give Jo Ann a ride?"

Jo Ann held her breath. This was all part of the plan. Mrs. Q. had to say yes.

"Yes," said Mrs. Q. "Of course I can."

Fifteen minutes later, they were ringing the doorbell at Jo Ann's house.

There were no extra cars on the street. And the house was quiet. Good, thought Jo Ann. Everything looks normal! But she could barely hold in her excitement.

Finally, Jo Ann's mom came to the door. "Thank you so much for bringing Jo Ann home," she said to Mrs. Q. "I've just made a fresh pot of coffee. Won't you come in?"

"Well, I really should be getting home," said Mrs. Q.

Jo Ann couldn't stand it anymore. "You can't go yet!" she said. "There's something you have to see!" She grabbed Mrs. Q.'s hand and towed her into the living room.

Mrs. Q. had one second to notice the banner and the decorations. Then the

Brownies jumped out of their hiding places.

"Surprise!" they shouted. "Happy birthday, Mrs. Q.!"

7

Mrs. Q.'s mouth was a big O. She looked totally surprised—and very, very happy.

The Brownies crowded around her, all talking at the same time. Finally she got a chance to speak. "I can't believe you did this!" she said. "You are amazing!"

"You didn't guess, did you?" Jo Ann said happily.

"We thought for sure you would—after you saw us at the party store," said Corrie.

"And after the way we acted at the meeting," added Marsha.

"I didn't have a clue," said Mrs. Q. "Although I did think you were acting pretty strange!"

The girls laughed.

"How did you know it was my birthday?" asked Mrs. Q. "I didn't tell anyone."

"Jo Ann saw the date on your time line," said Krissy S. "The surprise party was her idea."

"Thank you, Jo Ann!" Mrs. Q. gave her a big hug.

"You're welcome," said Jo Ann. "But it wasn't just me. We all did it together."

Amy put a gold crown on Mrs. Q.'s head. "I crown you Queen Q.!" she said with a bow.

"Here's your card, Mrs. Q.," said Corrie.

"And here's your present," said Lauren. "Happy birthday!"

Mrs. Q. opened them both. "Oh, my. Oh, my," she kept saying as she unfolded the card and turned the album pages. When she looked up, she had tears in her eyes.

"This is the best birthday a Brownie leader could have!" she said. "Thank you all!"

Just then the doorbell rang.

Could it be? thought Jo Ann. She ran to answer it.

Yes! It was Mr. Q. and Nina. Nina

looked just like her mom. Only she had dark hair, like her dad.

"Oh, Mrs. Q-oooo," Jo Ann called out in a teasing voice. "There are some people here to see you." Then she led the special guests into the living room.

Mrs. Q. jumped up. "You were in on this, too?" she asked, as she hugged and kissed her family. "It seems I'm surrounded by sneaky people!"

"Sneaky *hungry* people," said Amy. "Come on. Let's eat."

"Where's the chow? Where's the chow?" Cookie, the parrot, called loudly.

Jo Ann giggled. "It's in the dining room," she said. "Follow me, everyone!"

The Brownies crowded around the table. Jo Ann's sister Allison made sure everyone had a SURPRISE! plate and napkin. And her mom handed out cups of pineapple punch.

Jo Ann checked out the food. Everything looked good—especially the birthday cake. Krissy S. and her dad had done a super job.

There was only one thing missing. Jo Ann slipped into the kitchen to get it.

Nai-Nai was standing on tiptoe, taking a beautiful bowl from the cabinet. Jo Ann recognized it at once. It had been in the family for ages. Her grandmother only used it on very special days.

"Oh, Nai-Nai!" she said softly. "Is that for the almond dofu?"

"Yes," said Nai-Nai. "See the peaches on the sides? Peaches mean long life. And the peony flowers are for wealth and honor. Those are good birthday wishes, I think."

Jo Ann helped spoon the almond dofu into the bowl. "It looks beautiful, Nai-Nai," she said. "May I carry it into the dining room?"

Nai-Nai gave her a kiss. "Of course. Jo Ann do it self," she said. "I'll be right behind you."

Jo Ann felt very special carrying the Chinese bowl. She hoped the Brownies would like the almond dofu. Or at least try it. But no matter what they thought, she was glad she had made something she really loved.

Mrs. Q. peeked into the bowl as Jo Ann brought it in. "Mmmm! Is that almond dofu, Jo Ann? It looks delicious. Did you make it yourself?"

"My grandmother and I did," Jo Ann said proudly. She set the bowl on the table.

"I can't wait!" said Nina. She spooned some almond dofu into her cup.

"It really does look good," Krissy S. said. "Is that the stuff you were talking about?"

Jo Ann nodded.

"Can we try it?" asked Lauren and Amy.

"Sure," said Jo Ann. "I think you'll like it. It's my favorite."

Amy, Lauren, and Krissy helped themselves to some almond dofu. Amy took one bite. Then another. And another.

"Yum!" she said. "Can I have seconds?"

"Hey! Some of us haven't had firsts yet," said Corrie. She and the other Brownies lined up by the bowl.

Jo Ann grinned. She put a spoonful of almond dofu in her own cup. Then she went to get punch.

The next time she looked, the beautiful Chinese bowl was completely empty.

Girl Scout Ways

Jo Ann and her Brownie Girl Scout troop found out a lot about each other and themselves by making time lines of their lives. You can show all the ways that you are special, too, by making a time line of your very own.

- Here's what you'll need: crayons, markers or colored pencils, photographs of you and your family, tape or glue, and a long piece of paper with a line drawn down the middle and marked off in years.

- Beginning with zero (the day you were born), write down important things that have happened in your life. When did you learn to walk? When did you start school? When did you hit your first home run? Or have your first piano recital?

- Look in a scrapbook or baby book, just like Jo Ann did, for other special events that you might have forgotten. Or ask your family to help you out.

- Decorate your time line with photographs of you— or illustrate your time line with your own drawings.

- Time lines make great gifts, too! After you have finished your own time line, try making one for someone else in your family.